The Red Dragons of Gressingham

by

Philip Ardagh

Illustrated by Mike Phillips

In loving memory of Treasure,
a prince among goldfish

First published in 2012 in Great Britain by
Barrington Stoke Ltd
18 Walker St, Edinburgh, EH3 7LP

www.barringtonstoke.co.uk

4u2read edition based on *The Red Dragons of Gressingham*,
published by Barrington Stoke in 2008

ISBN: 978-1-78112-010-1

Printed in China by Leo

Contents

Chapter 1
The Big Yawn

Big Jim was bored. Fidget was bored. Friendly was bored. In fact, *all* of the Green Men of Gressingham were bored. They hung around the forest and yawned.

Fidget fidgeted. Friendly tried to make friends with an ant. Big Jim leaned on a tree. Big Jim was big, but the tree was bigger. Much bigger. It was the Green Men's look-out tree. When they were outlaws they used to go up it to look out for danger.

Now there was no danger to look out for. The Green Men had won their fight against evil Marshal Guppy. Lord Dashwood was back in charge at the Castle. All was quiet. The Green Men hung their washing on the look-out tree instead of going up it.

The roundest of the Green Men was Physic. He was busy hanging clothes on the tree to dry. The clothes were all brown. All the Green Men wore brown. Brown hid the dirt better than green, and they didn't wash their clothes *that* often.

"I'm so bored," said Physic as he hung the last brown sock on the tree.

"Me too," said Big Jim. "I wish some robbers would come to the forest and we could have a good old punch-up."

"We haven't had a punch-up for such a long time," said Fidget.

"Such a long, long, long, long, *long* time," said Friendly (he didn't like punch-ups much anyway).

"What about a bow-and-arrow contest?" said Lanky. He was almost as tall as Big Jim but very, very, *very* thin.

"We did that yesterday," Friendly said with a yawn.

"How about a pie-eating contest?" said Physic.

The other Green Men stared at Physic's great big tummy. "We did that the day *before* yesterday," said Big Jim.

"And you always win!" said Fidget.

Physic grinned. He loved pies.

"We could tidy the camp!" said Friendly. He had given up on the ant and was now trying to make friends with a buttercup.

"We are outlaws!" shouted Big Jim. "Outlaws don't do housework!"

"We're not outlaws any more," Friendly told him. "Now we are *in*-laws. We are on the same side as the law."

Big Jim frowned. "That's true," he said. "But I still don't like housework!"

"Bad luck," said Physic, "because it's your turn to feed Martha."

Martha was the Green Men's pet pig. She was big and very pink but it was hard to tell because she loved to roll in the mud. She looked as brown as the Green Men's clothes.

Big Jim got the bucket of food and went over to the pig pen. He said a few rude things but he didn't mind really. He was very fond of Martha.

The pig pen was empty.

"Martha has gone!" he shouted.

"Gone?" shouted the others.

"Gone!" said Big Jim.

The others rushed over to see.

Big Jim was right. The pig was gone.

Chapter 2
Under Attack

"How did Martha get out?" asked Friendly. "The gate is shut."

"Someone has stolen her!" said Physic. He was very upset. He loved Martha. He even looked a bit like her.

"You just said we could do with some robbers in the forest, Big Jim!" said Lanky.

"And now we've got some," said Fidget. "Pig robbers!"

The smallest of the Green Men was called Squat. He picked up a sword and waved it above his head. This wasn't hard because most things were above his head anyway. "We must find the robbers and get Martha back!" he shouted.

At that moment, something stung Squat's neck. He dropped the sword in shock. It stuck in the ground like King Arthur's sword in the stone. "Ouch!" he said.

"What's wrong?" asked Big Jim. Then something stung him on the cheek. "Ouch!!!" he shouted.

"What – ?" said Friendly. Then something stung *him* on the head.

"Shhh!" said Fidget. He pointed to a clump of bushes.

The Green Men stopped. Big Jim pulled the sword out of the ground. Lanky picked up his bow and arrows. Physic grabbed a big stick. Squat picked up a stone.

There were sounds coming from the bushes. They sounded like someone trying very hard not to laugh.

"Come on out!" shouted Big Jim. "With your hands up!"

A head popped out of the bushes. It was Tom, Lord Dashwood's nephew!

Tom was grinning from ear to ear. "Hello, everyone!" he said as he stood up. In one hand he was holding a piece of rope. In the other he had a pea-shooter.

"So that's what stung us!" Big Jim said. "You were shooting dried peas at us!"

"What a waste," Physic said. "They would make nice soup."

Tom laughed. "Trust you to think of your tummy, Physic!" he said. Then he pulled on the rope and Martha came out of the bushes. "Call yourself a bunch of outlaws?" Tom said. "I stole Martha from right under your noses."

"We're not really outlaws any more," Friendly said with a grin.

The Green Men were pleased to see Tom. He was a page boy, so they didn't see him very often. They all sat around the camp fire and Physic boiled a pot of water to make some nettle tea.

"How are things at the Castle, Tom?" asked Friendly.

"Will you be a knight soon?" asked Fidget.

"No." Tom sighed. "I'm beginning to think I'll be a page boy forever." Then he smiled. "But I have good news for you! Lord Dashwood has invited you all to the Castle!"

Chapter 3
To the Castle Once More

The Green Men left at once. That night they slept at *The Swan Inn*, under the sign of the blue bull. (Don't ask.) The following day, they set off again. They were met by a woman on a beautiful jet-black horse.

It was Robyn-in-the-Hat, the leader of the Green Men.

"Robyn!" shouted Tom. "It's good to see you again!"

"You too, Master Tom," Robyn said. She was called Robyn-in-the-Hat because of the funny hat she wore. It had a felt flap that came down over the top part of her face like a mask. There were two holes through which you could see her sparkling blue eyes.

Robyn used to wear the hat when the Green Men were outlaws so no one would know who she really was. Now that they were in-laws, people thought she would stop wearing it, but she didn't. "The secret must remain," she had said.

"Do you know what Lord Dashwood wants with us?" Robyn asked the Green Men. "Is Gressingham in danger again?"

"No," said Tom. "He said he has a surprise for you."

"And you don't know what it is?" Robyn asked.

Tom shook his head. "It will be a surprise for me too."

"I don't like surprises," said Fidget.

The soldier on look-out duty on the battlements of Dashwood Castle saw the Green Men long before they reached the castle gate. By the time they arrived, a small crowd was waiting to greet them. Tom's friend Able Morris was in the front wearing his favourite hat.

"Hello, Tom!" Able Morris said. "I see you found our fearless friends."

"Yes," said Tom. "And they are as keen as I am to find out what my uncle wants them for."

"They will find out very soon," said Able. "You are all to go to the Great Hall at once."

As soon as their horses had been taken to the stables, Tom led Robyn-in-the-Hat and the Green Men to the Great Hall. Lord Dashwood was sitting in a big wooden chair at the far end. He stood up when they came in.

"Welcome," he said. "I've been waiting for you!"

Chapter 4
The Plan Unfolds

"I want you to go to the Red Rock Mountains!" said Lord Dashwood. "You too, Tom."

Tom was amazed. "But no one goes to the Red Rock Mountains, Uncle!" he said.

"Not if they can help it," said Fidget.

"We'll need plenty of supplies, your lordship!" said Physic. He was already planning meals in his head.

"It could be – er – dangerous, sire," Friendly said.

"I thought you *liked* danger," said Lord Dashwood.

"Like it? We love it, my lord," said Robyn-in-the-Hat. Her eyes sparkled with excitement.

"There's just the small matter of the dragons," said Squat.

"Who said that?" asked Lord Dashwood.

Squat stepped out of Big Jim's big shadow. "I did, my Lord."

"And you think dragons are just a *small* matter?" said Lord Dashwood. He looked

around the great hall at all the other Green Men. "Well, if the smallest man among you thinks dragons are just a small matter, then I know I've chosen the right chaps for my quest!"

Squat wished he could say that he was only joking. He thought dragons might be a very big problem indeed. But then Lord Dashwood spoke.

"I want you to go to the Red Rock Mountains *and bring me back a dragon*," he said, with a big grin.

Now it wasn't just Tom who was amazed.

"A dragon quest!" said Robyn-in-the-Hat. "It will be an honour, my lord!"

"But what do you need a dragon for?" asked Friendly.

"Forgive the men, my lord," said Robyn. Tom guessed that she was frowning at Friendly behind her mask. "It will be an honour to bring you back a dragon."

"You did say *dragon*, didn't you, my lord?" asked Fidget. "One of those giant, fire-breathing monster things?"

"Just so," said Lord Dashwood with a nod.

"But don't they eat people?" asked Friendly. "I'm sure I heard somewhere that they eat people."

"My friend Baron Hankey has one," said Lord Dashwood. "He didn't say anything about it eating anybody."

"When do we start, my lord?" asked Big Jim. He thought anything was better than sitting around twiddling his thumbs.

"After a large meal?" Physic said hopefully.

Lord Dashwood's laughter boomed through the Hall. "What an excellent idea!" he said.

Chapter 5
Meet the Expert

After a very good meal, they made plans. There were no maps of the Red Rock Mountains. This was because so few people had been there. Or because the people who had gone there had never come back again. But there were maps showing the best ways to get to the mountains. The Green Men cleared the tables and laid these out.

"What's that wobbly line there?" Friendly asked.

"I think it's a stream," said Able Morris. He took a closer look at the map.

"And that big round thing?" asked Friendly.

"I think that's supposed to be a big rock," said Able Morris.

"And that thing which looks like a squashed fly?"

Tom scratched the mark on the map that Friendly was pointing at. "That *is* a squashed fly," he said.

"This map reading business is really easy!" said Friendly.

"I have asked a dragon expert to go with you on your quest," said Lord Dashwood. "His name is Dredwich." Lord Dashwood turned to Able Morris and spoke in his ear.

Able nodded his head and rushed out of the hall. His hat bobbed on the top of his head as he walked. He returned moments later with a man dressed in a dark, hooded robe. The man smelled of earth and old mushrooms.

The man bowed before Lord Dashwood. "This is Dredwich," Lord Dashwood said to the others.

"It is an honour to meet the Green Men of Gressingham," said Dredwich. "It is thanks to you that Marshal Guppy is now locked up where he belongs. I am pleased to be your servant and guide for this dangerous quest."

Big Jim slapped him on the back. "If you know *anything* about dragons then you know more about dragons than all the rest of us put together!" he said.

"I know they eat humans," said Friendly.

"And I know they are like big fire-breathing lizards," said Squat.

"A-ha," said Dredwich. "It seems you know a lot about dragons, in fact." He gave a wheezy cough.

"Are you a professional dragon expert?" Tom asked him.

"I am master of the unexplained and unexplainable," Dredwich said.

"What does that mean, sir?" Tom asked .

"I can't explain," said Dredwich. "Now, I must get ready for the dragon quest. Good day to you all." He left the room. There was a trail of soil where he had walked in and out.

"An odd fellow," said Big Jim.

"He smelled of old mushrooms," said Friendly.

"I like mushrooms," said Physic, which came as no surprise to anybody.

"Me too," said Tom.

Chapter 6
All Set to Go

Tom found it hard to sleep that night. A dragon quest! What could be more exciting? His tummy felt very funny. It was churning with a mix of excitement and fear.

Most of the others felt the same at breakfast. Very few ate more than a few mouthfuls, apart from Big Jim. The reason why Physic didn't eat anything was because he wasn't there. He had got up long before the others and gone down to the castle kitchens to make friends with the cook. By the time the rest came to breakfast, he had plenty of supplies for the quest. There were lots of sacks and barrels. All Physic had to do now was to find a way of carrying it all.

He found Tom after breakfast. "Will Lord Dashwood lend us three extra horses to carry our supplies?" he asked.

"I'm sure he will," Tom said. "After all, this is his special quest. I'll speak to Able about it."

Tom spoke to Able and Able spoke to Mr Nuzzle in the stables. Mr Nuzzle had a very important job. Knights couldn't be proper knights without horses, and horses needed looking after. That's what Mr Nuzzle did. He even looked like a horse.

Able Morris told Mr Nuzzle that the Green Men needed three more horses.

"I could offer them two horses and Stubborn," said Mr Nuzzle.

"Stubborn?" asked Able.

"Stubborn," said Mr Nuzzle.

"Isn't stubborn a mule?" Able asked.

"Yes, sire," said Mr Nuzzle. "But we only have two spare horses. And the mule."

A mule has a donkey for a father and a horse for a mother. There is a saying 'as stubborn as a mule'. Can you guess why that is? Yup. You're right. Mules can be very stubborn. They only do something if they want to do it.

If a mule is called Stubborn it must mean that it is a very stubborn mule indeed.

"That will have to do," Able said with a sigh. "Please get Stubborn and the two horses ready."

"Right away, sir," said Mr Nuzzle.

Chapter 7
Away at Last

Lord Dashwood was in his private room. He had a visitor.

"You are clear on your duties?" he asked Dredwich.

"Yes, your lordship," Dredwich said. "I must keep Robyn-in-the-Hat and the others away from the castle as long as possible."

"Exactly!" said Lord Dashwood. "I don't care what lies you tell them or false trails you lead them on, but you must keep them away from here at all costs. Do you understand?"

"I do, your lordship," said Dredwich. "Perfectly."

"Good luck," said Lord Dashwood.

Dredwich opened the door and walked out into the corridor, leaving his usual trail of soil behind him.

Many people in the castle came out to cheer off Robyn-in-the Hat, the Green Men (in brown), Tom and their guide. It wasn't every day that people set off on a quest to the Red Rock Mountains, let alone to bring back a dragon.

Suddenly there were three trumpet blasts and Lord Dashwood came out onto the

battlements. The crowds cheered. He put up his hands and made a short speech about the dangers ahead of the Green Men. When he had finished, the crowd cheered again. The gate was raised and the drawbridge was lowered across the moat. Robyn-in-the-Hat led the way on her fine black horse. Soon all that could be heard was the clatter of hooves on the bridge.

Stubborn the mule refused to move. Everyone stopped.

They pushed her.

They pulled her.

They even tried carrots.

In the end she did agree to follow the others but only as long as Friendly walked beside her, whispering into her ear.

Lord Dashwood made his way down the stone stairs. Able Morris was close behind.

"Now they're out of the way we can get down to the really important matters!" Lord Dashwood said.

Chapter 8
Strange Happenings

The first week of the dragon quest was a bit of a let-down. Everyone was keen to get to the mountains but the mountains were very far away. They passed through farms and towns and villages and got a great welcome wherever they went. Because they were on official business they were carrying a flag with the Dashwood coat of arms on it. The Dashwood coat of arms was a special design made for the Dashwood family. All Lord Dashwood's knights had it painted on their shields. That way, everyone knew that they were loyal to Lord Dashwood. The fact that the Green Men carried a flag with the coat of arms meant everyone knew they were under his protection.

Not that the Green Men needed protection. These were peaceful times. All of the lords were on friendly terms at the time of the dragon quest. In one village, a group of children did throw vegetables at them but Physic was delighted. He jumped down off his horse and picked them up in his arms.

"These will make good soup!" he said.

Apart from that, the only other bit of excitement was on the fourth day. That was when some locals were foolish enough to try to rob them. Before the robbers knew what was happening, Big Jim had knocked two of them over with his stick. Physic was sitting on another one, and four more were being

tied up by the other Green Men. All the
robbers were left in a pile by the road
wishing that they had chosen any career
other than robbery.

When the first week was over things got
more interesting. It was time to use the maps
and get off the beaten track. Now the Green
Men wouldn't be following paths at all.

The mountains were still far off but now they were beginning to look a bit closer. Now they could see the redness of the rocks that gave the mountains their name.

The next night they made camp in a place that was called *Ye Woods* on the map but which was more like a big clump of trees. (Tom read the map – he could read quite a few words and write his own name.)

Physic made a meal over the campfire and the others stared into the flames and talked about dragons.

"Grubs up!" said Physic.

"Excellent!" said Big Jim. "What is it? I'm starving!"

"I just told you," said Physic. "It's grubs. Grub stew!"

All of a sudden Tom didn't feel so hungry. Grubs were like small white worms. He decided to go to bed hungry.

Chapter 9
The Red Rocks

The next day the Green Men reached the foot-hills of the mountains. There were a lot of smiles and cheers and Physic gave everyone an extra bun. He had made them a while ago so they were quite stale. Very stale, in fact. They were almost as hard as some of the small red rocks at their feet.

"I nearly broke a tooth!" Big Jim moaned. He threw his bun at Physic. It was lucky it

missed him. It could have done the ex-outlaw some real damage!

"They're not that bad," said Friendly, who wanted to be friendly. (The truth be told, he couldn't get his teeth into his either.)

"Forget the buns!" shouted Squat. "What's that?" He pointed up the mountain.

Tom tried to work out exactly where the smallest of the Green Men was pointing. He couldn't see anything at first, just plenty of rocks and a few trees. Then he saw it – a puff of smoke, half-way up the mountain.

"There must be someone up there!" said Tom.

"Or *something*," groaned Fidget. He started to fidget. "That could be dragon smoke."

"Could that be dragon's breath?" Big Jim asked Dredwich.

"It could be," said Dredwich from inside the hood of his cloak. At first, he sounded unsure. Then he sounded a bit keener. "Most probably," he said. "In truth, most definitely. Indeed! A very fine example, in fact."

"So we can take that as a yes?" said Tom.

"Yes," said Dredwich the so-called dragon expert. "We're on the right track!"

"Come on, then!" said Big Jim. "Let's catch ourselves a dragon!"

Chapter 10
Where Be Dragons?

Now, *you* know that there are dragons in this story and *I* know that there are dragons in this story. There is the word 'dragons' in the title and there are even some pictures of dragons on the cover. But the Green Men of Gressingham could not find any dragons at all. They searched for days. And nights. They climbed high into the mountains and deep into the valleys. They searched in caves and looked behind big rocks. Dredwich kept on finding 'clues' that none of the others saw or understood. He led them here, there and everywhere for days on end.

And what did they find? Nothing. Not a sausage. (Physic would have been pleased with a sausage or two. They were running out of supplies.)

In the end, Robyn called them all together. "We have done our best," she said. "No one can do more. It is time to return to Lord Dashwood and tell him we've failed."

Tom was feeling very flat. He had failed his first quest!

"Not to worry," said Dredwich, who seemed quite cheerful. "If there were any dragons here we would have found them. I'm sure Lord Dashwood will understand that. It will be good to get back to the Castle."

"I can't say that I mind not having come face to face with a fire-breathing man-eating monster," Squat said.

"Call yourself an outlaw?" Big Jim asked.

"An *in*-law," Lanky said. "We act within the law now, remember?"

Everyone put a brave face on it, but the Green Men began their long ride home with heavy hearts.

Physic and Friendly collected a few of the strange small round rocks which covered the mountain side. Each was about the size and shape of a football (although they didn't know

that as no one would get around to inventing
the game until hundreds of years later).

"What do you want those for?" asked Tom.

"They'll make good presents," said
Friendly.

"And they'll be proof that we actually went to the Red Rock Mountains," Fidget added. The rocks were a very strange red colour indeed.

"And few people can claim to have been to these mountains and come back alive!" said Big Jim. The thought seemed to cheer him up.

"And I've made a map of everywhere we went," said Tom. "That's never been done before either!"

"So we've much to be proud of, even if we don't return with a dragon," said Robyn. She always tried to be as positive as possible.

Even less happened on the journey back than on the way there. Most of the villages they passed were oddly empty. When Dashwood Castle came into view days later, there was no one to welcome them.

"I'm glad about that," said Fidget. "The fewer people who see us come back without a dragon, the better."

"I shall ride ahead and tell Lord Dashwood that you failed," said Dredwich.

"We failed?" said Big Jim. "You failed too, Dredwich."

"And you're the expert," muttered Physic.

"Er, yes. Quite," said Dredwich. He kicked his horse and rode off to the castle.

Chapter 11
A Wild Goose Chase?

When the rest of the Green Men arrived back at the castle, they were in for a surprise. As they went through the gate into the court-yard they couldn't believe their eyes. There were flags and banners and pennants everywhere. The hooves of their horses were silent as there was a thick carpet laid over the cobble-stones. Lord Dashwood himself was rushing down the steps towards them.

"Welcome! Welcome!" Lord Dashwood beamed. He opened his arms wide.

Robyn-in-the-Hat jumped off her fine black horse and bowed. "Dredwich has told you that we failed, my lord?" she asked.

Lord Dashwood smiled. "You did not fail," he said. "It is more correct to say that Dredwich succeeded."

"I don't understand, Uncle," said Tom.

"The dragon quest was a wild goose chase," Lord Dashwood said. "A trick to get you away from the castle."

"You didn't really want a dragon?" said Tom.

"I would love a dragon, but I'm not even sure that they exist!" said his uncle.

"But what about the dragon expert, sire?" asked Robyn.

"Dredwich?" said Lord Dashwood. "He is no dragon expert. He is my friend Baron Hankey's gardener! I had him play the part."

"A gardener!" said Tom. "That explains the smell of mushrooms and the trail of soil! But why did you want us out of the way, Uncle?"

"So that we could get ready," Lord Dashwood said.

"Get ready? Get ready for what, your lordship?" asked Big Jim.

"For your reward for saving me from evil Marshal Guppy," said Lord Dashwood.

"Are you going to have another feast?" asked Physic. He had good memories of the last one.

"There will indeed be a feast, Physic," Lord Dashwood said, "You can be sure of that. But I want to reward you all in a more lasting way, now that I am fully well again."

"How, Uncle?" asked Tom.

"You are to be a squire, Tom. You will no longer be just a page boy. You have worked hard and you deserve the title."

Tom glowed with pride.

"The rest of you – " Lord Dashwood stopped and looked at Big Jim, Physic, Fidget, Squat, Lanky and the others. "You are to become my knights."

The Green Men's mouths all fell open.

"All of the people from miles around have come here for your special day," said Lord Dashwood. "It will be tomorrow."

Just then there was a cry from Friendly, who had just reached the castle. He had been walking next to Stubborn the mule, who could only walk very slowly because he was carrying the heavy round red rocks.

"One's hatching!" Friendly shouted.

"Hatching?" said Tom.

"Hatching!" shouted Friendly. He held up one of the football-shaped red rocks. It did, indeed, seem to be hatching.

A moment later, the top of the rock broke off and out poked the head of a tiny dragon.

Yup. You read that right. *Out poked the head of a tiny dragon.*

The little dragon flapped its tiny wings and flew up into the air. It made a sound like a sneeze and flames shot out of its nose!

A guard ran through the gate. "They're all hatching, my lord!" he shouted. He was trying to fight off a number of bat-sized baby dragons.

The dragons swooped. They looped-the-loop. They dive-bombed the people in the court-yard below. They sneezed and breathed out fire.

"Awww!" said Physic. "Aren't they sweet?"

"Arrgh!!" shouted Tom as one of them burned his bottom.

Big Jim had tiny dragons flying around his head like a swarm of bees. He laughed a big

laugh. "We did it, Robyn," he said. "We brought back dragons!"

Just then, one of the baby red dragons landed on Tom's arm and began to bite his ear.

Lord Dashwood roared with laughter too. "I don't believe it!" he said. "Only the Green Men of Gressingham could go on a wild goose chase and actually catch the goose!"

An Afterword

And so it was that Tom became a squire and each of the Green Men became a knight: Sir Jim, Sir Physic, Sir Friendly, Sir Squat, Sir Lanky and so on. Lord Dashwood also gave the Green Men some land to go with their titles. He gave them Gressingham Forest.

Robyn-in-the-Hat would not take any title or reward. How could she, when no one knew who she was? For all they knew, she could already have a title of her own.

The Green Men went on many more quests, but Sir Fidget and Sir Friendly often stayed behind. They had an important job of their own. The two knights (and Stubborn the mule) looked after more than twenty little ones – the famous Red Dragons of Gressingham.

Our books are tested
for children and young people by
children and young people.

Thanks to everyone who consulted on
a manuscript for their time and effort in
helping us to make our books better
for our readers.

Find out how the Green Men went from outlaws, to inlaws, in...

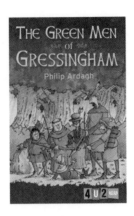

The Green Men of Gressingham

by Philip Ardagh

The Green Men are outlaws, living in a forest. Now they have taken Tom prisoner! What do they want from him? Who is their secret leader, Robyn-in-the-Hat? And whose side should Tom be on?